THE
IRELANDOPEDIA
QUIZ
BOOK

AN *'Ask Me Questions'* BOOK

BAINTE DEN STOC

SHAUNA BURKE

GILL BOOKS

Gill Books
Hume Avenue
Park West
Dublin 12
www.gillbooks.ie

Gill Books is an imprint of M.H. Gill and Co.

Text © Shauna Burke 2017
Illustrations © Kathi 'Fatti' Burke 2017

978 07171 7863 6

Print origination by Jen Patton
Printed by CPI Group (UK) Ltd, CR0 4YY

This book is typeset in Brandon Grotesque and Wanderlust.

The paper used in this book comes from the wood pulp of managed forests. For every tree felled, at least one tree is planted, thereby renewing natural resources.

A CIP catalogue record for this book is available from the British Library.

5 4 3

About the Author

Shauna Burke is a full-time secondary school teacher from Co. Waterford. She teaches English and Religion in St Angela's Secondary School, where she was also a student! She studied English and Religious Education in Mater Dei Institute of Education and graduated in 2014. She has a passion for table quizzes, trivia and telling stories. She is also the sister and daughter of illustrator and author duo Fatti and John Burke!

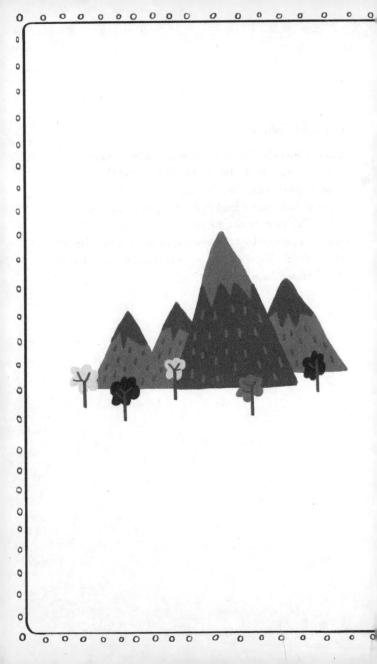

QUESTIONS

Quiz

1

Round 1

1. What county beginning with 'M' is known as the drumlin county?

2. The Nobel Prize-winning poet Seamus _____ attended St Columb's college in Co. Derry.

3. Yellowman, sold in Co. Antrim, is a type of: a) footwear b) sweet c) garden tool.

4. *Seilide* is the Irish for what slimy-shelled creature?

5. Poc Fada is a long-distance style of what GAA sport?

6. What is the capital of the Republic of Ireland?

7. The remains of which romantic saint are buried in Whitefriar Street Church in Dublin?

8. What province is Co. Wicklow in?

9. What mythical couple are said to be buried at Benbulbin in Co. Sligo?

10. The most northerly point in Ireland is called _____ Head.

Round 2

1. In Co. Mayo, there is a National Museum of _____ Life.

2. What floating mode of transportation once crashed into the town of Tullamore?

3. Spell 'Laois', the county in Leinster.

4. James Martin, born in Co. Down, invented the: a) ejection seat b) telescope c) cornflake.

5. John B. Keane, from Co. Kerry, wrote a play called *The* _____, about two men fighting over farmland.

6. There is a festival in Longford town every September celebrating what stringed instrument?

7. On what date do people from the country traditionally travel to Dublin to do their Christmas shopping?

8. James Farrell from Co. Longford saved the lives of two girls on what famous sinking ship?

9. What comedian and television host, known for hosting *Mock the Week*, was born in Bray, Co. Wicklow? D____ O'B_____.

10. The king of Ireland was crowned on what hill in Co. Meath? Hint: It's also a woman's name!

Round 3

1. What type of sweaters are special to the Galway area?

2. The penalty kick was invented by: a) George Best b) William McCrum c) Lionel Messi.

3. There is a museum and heritage centre in Limerick dedicated to former President and Taoiseach, Éamon __ ____.

4. Monasterevin in Co. Kildare is also known as 'The ____ of Ireland' because it has many bridges, just like the city in Italy.

5. What is said to be buried under the Rock of Dunamase in Laois? Hint: Pirates are known for burying this!

6. In Fermanagh, there is a meaty delicacy known as Black ____.

7. Coumshingaun in Co. Waterford is a fine example of a type of what?

8. What is the Irish word for milk?

9. The only two Gaeltacht areas in Leinster, Baile Ghib and Ráth Cairn, are found in which county?

10. What famous golfer comes from Holywood in Co. Down?

Round 4

1. Name the only county in Ireland beginning with 'R'.

2. Bulmers, which comes from Clonmel in Co. Tipperary, is a type of: a) cider b) cola c) whiskey.

3. Name the singer-songwriter born in Co. Dublin, best known for her song 'Nothing Compares 2 U': _____ O'Connor.

4. In what Leinster county would you find the town of Muine Bheag?

5. What Irish sporting organisation was founded by Michael Cusack?

6. Pilgrims travel to what town in Co. Mayo to honour the Virgin Mary?

7. In which county in Connacht would you find Carrowmore, the biggest megalithic site in Ireland?

8. John Joe Nevin, born in Mullingar, is known for what Olympic sport?

9. Rissoles, sold in chippers in Wexford, are a type of fried: a) chocolate bar b) potato cake c) sausage.

10. Lugnaquilla is the highest point in which mountain range? W_____ Mountains.

Round 5

1. What Olympic medal-winning female runner was born in Cobh, Co. Cork?

2. Mount Brandon in Co. Kerry is a popular spot for: a) golfers b) bird watchers c) pilgrims.

3. Margaret Haughery is known for opening what in New Orleans to help children?

4. In which county would you find Loftus Hall, one of the most haunted places in Ireland?

5. Who wrote the novel *Gulliver's Travels*? Jonathan ____.

6. What fizzy drink do Irish people drink flat when they're sick?

7. The Bridge of Tears in Limerick was a famous place to say goodbye when people were emigrating to where?

8. Spell 'dolmen', a type of megalithic tomb.

9. What city in Antrim is musician Van Morrison from?

10. What mythological Irish hero is said to have tied himself to a standing stone at Knockbridge as he was dying? C____n.

Quiz

2

Round 1

1. What Munster county was the GAA started in?

2. What type of buzzing insects would you find in an apiary?

3. *Camán* is the Irish for what piece of sporting equipment?

4. What well-known crisps are made in Tandragee in Co. Armagh?

5. The Lambert Puppet Theatre in Monkstown made a children's TV series about which red-haired puppet?

6. Which of the following was **NOT** found in the Bog of Allen: a) a canoe b) a jewellery box c) butter.

7. There is a festival in Granard celebrating what stringed musical instrument which is also found on Irish money?

8. Which park is home to Dublin Zoo?

9. A goosander is: a) a fish b) a duck c) an insect.

10. People from which county are nicknamed 'The Cats'?

Round 2

1. A type of polo was invented in Co. Wicklow where the players ride on what instead of horses?

2. Carrickmacross is well known for making what type of pretty fabric?

3. What football player, born in Rathfarnham, has played for Newcastle United, Chelsea, Fulham, Blackburn Rovers and the Republic of Ireland?

4. What Ulster county has the slogan 'Up here it's different'?

5. What do you call the floury bread bun eaten in Waterford?

6. In which county might you be able to attend a Pork Festival and witness the *Olympigs*?

7. What famous landmark in Co. Antrim is made of 40,000 rock columns?

8. In Lough Ree there have been sightings of:
a) a monster b) a mermaid c) a whale.

9. What is the Irish word for bread?

10. The owner of The King's Head pub in Galway once did an unpleasant task for Oliver Cromwell. What did he do?

Round 3

1. In what county beginning with 'W' would you find the longest handmade stone bridge in Ireland?

2. What town in Mayo was voted the best place to live in Ireland and has won the Tidy Towns competition many times? W_____.

3. What province is Waterford in?

4. What is the name of the Dublin-born mixed martial artist and UFC champion?

5. What type of fruit is a Bramley's Seedling?

6. Belfast-born writer C.S. Lewis wrote *The Chronicles of* ____.

7. What animal is Tipperary famous for breeding?

8. Which waterfall rises in the Devil's Punchbowl in Co. Kerry? T___ Waterfall.

9. Who shows up to weddings in the West wearing straw masks?

10. What should you kiss to receive the 'Gift of the Gab'?

Round 4

1. What is the only county with a 'V' in its name?

2. What popular music festival takes place in Stradbally Estate in Laois every summer?

3. In what county would you find Mullyash Mountain?

4. Football Special is a type of: a) TV show b) fizzy drink c) sports shop.

5. The ancestors of what famous mouse-loving animator are buried in Ballyloo, Co. Carlow?

6. Glendalough is in what county?

7. Spell 'Tipperary'.

8. Which island is the biggest of the Aran Islands? a) Inis Mór b) Inis Meáin c) Inis Oírr.

9. How many provinces are there in Ireland?

10. Which famous festival for Irish women around the world is celebrated in Tralee every year?

Round 5

1. What type of dog was Fury, who saved the life of a child in Portumna castle?

2. Joe Dolan was a pop singer from what county?

3. What water sport is very popular in Bundoran, Co. Donegal?

4. What famous Irish saint worked as a shepherd on Slemish Mountain?

5. What is the name of the stadium in Dublin where Ireland's rugby games are played?

6. The town of Castlebar is in what Connacht county?

7. A kittiwake is a type of: a) flower b) rodent c) bird.

8. The Dunbrody Famine Ship is found in which county?

9. It is said that the Rock of Cashel was made when Satan took a bite out of a mountain and spat it away. What was the name of the mountain? D____ B__ Mountain.

10. Meath is Ireland's leading producer of what crop? Hint: It's very popular with Mr Tayto!

Quiz

3

Round 1

1. Which city in Ulster is the most complete walled city in Europe?

2. What famous Irish writer is known for his books *Ulysses*, *Dubliners* and *Finnegans Wake*? J____ J____.

3. In what county would you find Reginald's Tower?

4. According to legend, a king in Loughmore Castle offered his daughter's hand in marriage in exchange for: a) killing a boar b) swimming to Wales c) baking a pie.

5. Who was born in Callan, Co. Kilkenny, and was the founder of the Christian Brothers? Hint: His last name is a type of food! Edmund ____.

6. What county is home to Aillwee Cave?

7. What famous song was written about the Athenry area?

8. Turlough O'Carolan, who was blind, was famous for playing what instrument?

9. Tayto Park in Co. Meath is home to Ireland's first herd of what American animal?

10. Oliver Goldsmith from Co. Longford made up what term, describing someone who always follows the rules and does everything right?

Round 2

1. The city of Newry is split between what two counties? A____ and D__.

2. A yew is a type of: a) drink b) tree c) boat.

3. There is a competition in Freshford, Co. Kilkenny, called the Irish C____ Championships. Hint: You need some horse chestnuts to take part!

4. What Waterford company was the very first maker of cream crackers?

5. The devil is said to have visited Loftus Hall in Co. Wexford. What did he leave in the roof?

6. In what city is a Jazz Festival held every October?

7. What date is St Patrick's Day?

8. *Mála tae* is the Irish for what essential kitchen item?

9. Which well-known poet comes from Monaghan? Patrick _____.

10. What is the name of Ireland's National GAA Stadium?

Round 3

1. Andrea, Sharon, Caroline and Jim are siblings in what famous family music act from Louth?

2. In what county would you find the Mermaid Stones of Scurmore?

3. How many counties in Ireland start with 'C'?

4. The first Irish tricolour flag was raised in what county?

5. Phil Lynott was the frontman of which Dublin band? Hint: Skinny Elizabeth!

6. What is the name of W. B. Yeats' brother, who was a famous artist?

7. The ferry service in Rosslare brings people to what two countries?

8. *Colúr* is Irish for what type of city-living bird?

9. What is Ireland's main centre for water sports, found in Co. Dublin? National _____ Centre.

10. The River Shannon begins in which county?

Round 4

1. Lilliput House in Co. Westmeath was used by which author as a holiday home? Jonathan ____.

2. A gillaroo is a type of: a) trout b) rabbit c) lizard.

3. What guitarist and songwriter is remembered with a statue in his hometown of Ballyshannon? Rory G_____.

4. The city of Belfast is mostly in what county?

5. Puck Fair in Killorglan crowns a mountain ____ as king of the town every year.

6. New Ross is in what county?

7. What type of dog is Mick the Miller, who has his own statue in Offaly?

8. Darren Clarke from Dungannon in Co. Tyrone is a professional in what sport?

9. In which county would you find Tullynally castle?

10. What is the biggest town in Donegal? L_____y.

Round 5

1. Which county in Ulster is Ireland's second biggest producer of crystal?

2. Physicist John Tyndall is famous for explaining: a) why the sky is blue b) why birds can fly c) why grass is green.

3. The town of Tullamore is in what county in Leinster?

4. What bumpy skin infection is St Patrick's Well in Tyrone supposed to be good at healing?

5. True or false: Cupidstown Hill is the highest point in Kildare.

6. In which county was Michael D. Higgins born?

7. What meat product, usually eaten at breakfast, was developed in Waterford by Henry Denny in 1820?

8. What TV show do Irish people stay up to watch and find out about the latest toys for Christmas?

9. Carnagh East is a town in the very centre of Ireland – what county is it in?

10. Spell 'Fermanagh'.

Quiz
4

Round 1

1. Which Gaelic games commentator comes from Dún Síon in Co. Kerry? _____ Ó Muircheartaigh.

2. Former US presidents Ulysses S. Grant and Woodrow Wilson had ancestors from what Irish county?

3. What breed of dog hails from Kerry and is used for hunting and guarding your home? Kerry _____ Terrier.

4. What is the name of the comedy festival that takes place annually in Kilkenny?

5. How many counties beginning with 'A' are there in Ireland?

6. Oliver Goldsmith is a novelist and playwright from which county in Leinster?

7. A traditional music festival held in Monaghan every May has a competition for players of what stringed instrument?

8. What is the highest hill in Co. Westmeath, but the lowest county top in the country?

9. Glencar Waterfall in Co. Leitrim was mentioned in a poem by what Irish poet? W. B. ____.

10. 'Poke' is a word used in Co. Down for what type of sweet treat, often eaten by the seaside?

Round 2

1. Which county in Ireland has the shortest coastline?

2. Neil Jordan from Co. Sligo directed what film about a famous Irish nationalist leader? M_____ C_____.

3. On a clear day, what country can you see from the top of the Great Sugarloaf?

4. Shellakybooky is a Waterford name for what slimy, shelled animal?

5. The grounds of what castle in Co. Meath have been used to host rock concerts since 1981?

6. A Little Tern is: a) a frog b) a bird c) a cake.

7. Which river runs through Galway city? River C_____.

8. In what county in Ulster is Belleek Pottery made?

9. Christy Moore wrote a song about a town that also holds a matchmaking event every year. Name the town.

10. What famous ship was built in the Harland and Wolff shipyard in Belfast?

Round 3

1. Who is the lead singer of the Dublin band U2?

2. *Éala* is the Irish word for what graceful bird?

3. How many counties are there in Ulster?

4. Michael Davitt, who started the National Land League, was from which county?

5. When the waters of Lough Allen are low, you can see: a) treasure b) crannogs c) eels.

6. Marble Arch was home to what extinct giant animal? Hint: It was much bigger than Bambi!

7. What do Dubliners call the Natural History Museum? The ___ Zoo.

8. According to legend, who built the Giant's Causeway?

9. Armagh is the only city in the world with two cathedrals of the same name. They are both called St _____.

10. Mondello Park is Ireland's only international venue for what sport?

Round 4

1. In what county would you find Croagh Patrick, where many people go on pilgrimages?

2. Falmouth Kearney from Moneygall was the great-great-great grandfather of which US president?

3. What apple-flavoured fizzy drink was first made in Clonmel, Co. Tipperary?

4. What is the longest river in Ireland?

5. The hibernation den of the brown _____ can be found in Aillwee Cave.

6. What Irish city in Ulster is also known as Stroke City?

7. Rev. James McDonald was an ancestor of Rudyard Kipling, who wrote a book about Mowgli and Baloo the bear. Name the book.

8. What sport takes place in Punchestown racecourse?

9. Name the ninth president of Ireland, born in Limerick, who is also a poet, sociologist and author.

10. What world-famous brooch was found on a beach in Bettystown?

Round 5

1. Mullingar is a town in what Leinster county?

2. What is the Irish word for cheese?

3. Peter O'Toole, born in Connemara, starred in the film *Lawrence of _____*?

4. In which county was Ireland's first Lifeboat Station set up?

5. How many Gaeltacht areas are there in Co. Cork?

6. John Philip Holland from Co. Clare is known for inventing: a) the hot air balloon b) the kayak c) the submarine.

7. What boxing champion comes from Bray, Co. Wicklow?

8. In which city is the book *Angela's Ashes* by Frank McCourt set?

9. What castle in Kildare was built in the 13th century as home to the FitzGerald family?

10. The Ox Mountains are found in which county?

Quiz 5

Round 1

1. Charles Stewart _____ was born in Rathdrum, Co. Wicklow, and has a memorial park dedicated to him.

2. How many bridges are there in Cork city? a) 38 b) 29 c) 16.

3. What is Ireland's most visited natural attraction? Hint: You have to keep away from the edge!

4. How many counties are there in Munster?

5. Which of these is **NOT** a type of duck? a) wigeon b) indigo c) teal.

6. Athenry is a town in what county?

7. What can you find in Birr, Co. Offaly, that you can use to look at the stars?

8. What boyband singer comes from Mullingar, Co. Westmeath?

9. What date is St Brigid's Day?

10. The Slieve Aughty mountains spread from Galway into what county?

Round 2

1. Torpey is the leading brand of what piece of GAA equipment?

2. What hot drink was invented by Sir Hans Sloane from Killyleagh?

3. In what county would you find St Mel's Cathedral?

4. How many counties in Ireland start with 'D'?

5. The Céide Fields in Co. Mayo are the remains of a farming community from the _____ Age.

6. What seafood is celebrated with a festival in Clarenbridge, Co. Galway?

7. The heart of St Laurence O'Toole can be found in _____ Church Cathedral.

8. What county's GAA team is nicknamed The Scallion Eaters?

9. What river runs through Cork city?

10. Which famous leader appeared on the Irish £20 note and has a street named after him in Dublin city? Daniel _____.

Round 3

1. True or false: Visitors go to Newgrange on the summer solstice every year to see the inner chambers light up.

2. What museum in Roscommon remembers a very hungry time in Irish history? Irish National F_____ Museum.

3. Brian Friel, the playwright born in Tyrone, wrote a play called _____ at Lughnasa?

4. In what Leinster county would you find Powerscourt House, which has beautiful walled gardens?

5. Which of these rivers does **NOT** flow through Kildare? a) River Barrow b) River Liffey c) River Boyne.

6. Veda, a food popular in Northern Ireland, is a type of: a) bread b) meat pie c) creamy dessert.

7. Which airport has the longest runway in Ireland?

8. In what county beginning with 'C' would you find over 360 lakes?

9. What is the Irish word for bridge?

10. Ireland's first bottled mineral water was made in what county?

Round 4

1. What are crubeens made from?

2. Percy French wrote a song called 'Come Back Paddy Reilly to Ballyjamesduff' about: a) his brother b) his doctor c) his driver.

3. Bushmills is known for what type of alcoholic drink?

4. What famous female pilot landed just outside Derry city on her solo transatlantic flight? _____ Earheart.

5. How many counties are there in Leinster?

6. What festival celebrating something used to frighten birds is celebrated in Co. Laois?

7. The Ardagh Chalice was found by two boys in: a) a river b) a football pitch c) a potato field.

8. What famous female saint is believed to have been born in Faughart, Co. Louth?

9. Which of these is **NOT** a type of bird? a) crossbill b) guppy c) whimbrel.

10. What castle in Co. Offaly is one of the most haunted castles in Ireland? L___ Castle.

Round 5

1. In what Leinster county would you find a haunted gaol?

2. William Jacob started making what type of food in Waterford in 1851?

3. What Sligo-born actress played the role of tea-loving Mrs Doyle in *Father Ted*?_____ McLynn.

4. What village in Limerick has been called Ireland's prettiest village?

5. What dairy manufacturer has its headquarters on the edge of Kilkenny city? Hint: Its name in Irish means 'clean food'.

6. Spell 'Monaghan'.

7. Ken Doherty is a world professional champion in what sport?

8. The corkscrew-shaped barn found in Co. Kildare is called: a) The Brilliant Barn b) The Wonderful Barn c) The Pretty Great Barn.

9. What is the home ground of Munster Rugby?

10. What is the name of the home of Lady Gregory, co-founder of the Abbey Theatre? C___ Park.

Quiz

6

Round 1

1. Three members of which famous boyband were born in Sligo?

2. In what county might you hear a person say 'This is me, is that you?' when answering the phone?

3. The Lady of the Lake is a mythical figure found in: a) Lough Erne b) Lough Arrow c) Loch Ness.

4. What brand of crisps has its own theme park in Co. Meath?

5. Which canal goes from Dublin to Abbeyshrule in Longford?

6. What famous cinematic lion was born in Dublin Zoo?

7. In which county in Ulster could you attend Europe's biggest Bob Dylan music festival?

8. What popular folk singer, known for songs such as *Lisdoonvarna* and *Don't Forget Your Shovel*, is from Kildare? Christy ____.

9. Glen Lough Nature Reserve has a large number of what bird? Whooper ____.

10. Birr Castle Estate is home to the largest ____ in Ireland: a) see-saw b) maze c) tree house.

Round 2

1. The water in St Feichin's Well, Co. Westmeath, is special because it will not _____?

2. What Leinster county holds Ireland's longest-running air show?

3. What restaurant and cookery school in Co. Cork is famous for its yummy relish?

4. What cosmic material landed in a potato field in Clonoulty in 1865?

5. What unusual championships, which take place in Castleblayney, involve swimming in a trench? Irish B__ S_____ Championships.

6. The Cliffs of Moher are found in which county?

7. What famous Irish king is said to be buried in Armagh? B__ B__.

8. Clouded yellow, red admiral and painted lady are all types of what fluttering insect?

9. In which Connacht county could you play a tune on the Musical Bridge?

10. A bonham is a young: a) pig b) sheep c) duck.

Round 3

1. What is the name of the official home of the President of Ireland?

2. How many counties are there in Connacht?

3. The Marble Arch Caves are in counties Cavan and _____?

4. Which famous nationalist leader was from Clonakilty in Co. Cork? Michael _____.

5. What seafood is celebrated with a festival on Valentia Island? a) scallops b) prawns c) scampi.

6. Architect James Hoban designed which famous building in Washington DC?

7. In what town would you find Co. Cork's only horse-racing course?

8. In which county would you find the Dartry Mountains?

9. What town in Mayo has its own airport?

10. Carlingford is a town in what Leinster county?

Round 4

1. What mountain is considered the holiest in Ireland? Croagh ____.

2. Ardal O'Hanlon from Monaghan played which simple-minded character in the TV show *Father Ted*?

3. Roscommon is Ireland's biggest producer of what meat?

4. Laurence Sterne, author of *The Life and Opinions of Tristram Shandy, Gentleman*, is from what county beginning with 'T'?

5. 'Red Lead' is another name for what type of sandwich meat?

6. There is an arboretum in Co. Wexford named after US president John F. Kennedy. What would you find in an arboretum?

7. What is the Irish word for sausages?

8. What is the capital city of Northern Ireland?

9. True or false: Pierce Butler from Co. Carlow signed the American Constitution.

10. In what Munster county would you find Loop Head?

Round 5

1. What mountain range is found in Derry? a) Slieve Bernagh Mountains b) Slieve Bloom Mountains c) Sperrin Mountains.

2. What important farming vehicle was invented by Harry Ferguson of Co. Down?

3. Fionn mac Cumhaill's Irish wolfhounds were said to be turned into what by a witch? a) mountains b) rabbits c) hurleys.

4. What famous aquatic mammal lives in Dingle, Co. Kerry?

5. Naas is the county town of what county?

6. What female chef and food writer was born in Cullohill, Co. Laois? Darina ____.

7. The Hunt Museum in Limerick city contains art by what famous Spanish modern artist? Pablo _____.

8. Dermot O'Brien was a musician who also played what sport?

9. Name the famous passage tomb found in Co. Meath.

10. In which Leinster county would you find the Irish Parachute Club?

Quiz 7

Round 1

1. Chris O'Dowd from Co. Roscommon stars in the comedy TV show _____ Boy.

2. Mullaghmore is one of the best locations in the world for what water sport?

3. Castlederg, Co. Tyrone, hosts a fair every year for what type of fruit?

4. Sean's Bar in Athlone is famous for being:
a) the smallest pub in Ireland b) the oldest pub in Europe c) the cheapest pub in the world.

5. Eddie Jordan, who grew up in Bray, is known for what sport?

6. What vegetable was traditionally used in Ireland for carving faces on Halloween?

7. _Sútha talún_ is the Irish for what sweet berries?

8. What is the name of the river that runs through Dublin city?

9. What county in Ulster is also known as 'The Orchard County'?

10. What kind of animal is the goldeneye? a) bird b) dog c) fish.

Round 2

1. In which county in Munster would you find the holiday village of Trabolgan?

2. True or false: Killybegs is the smallest fishing port in Ireland.

3. What Dalkey-born author wrote *Circle of Friends* and *Tara Road*? Maeve B____.

4. What breed of pony, bred in Galway, has its own show every August?

5. Which county does Newbridge Silverware come from?

6. Frank McCourt, born in Limerick, wrote what book based on his childhood? *Angela's A____*.

7. Spell 'Connacht'.

8. What famous actor, known for his role as James Bond, grew up in Navan? ____ Brosnan.

9. Brian O'Nolan, the novelist and playwright, wrote under what name? F____ O'Brien.

10. 'Well that beats Banagher!' is a phrase referring to a town in which county?

Round 3

1. The Lily Lolly Craftfest in Sligo celebrates Susan and Elizabeth, sisters of which famous Irish poet? W. B. ____.

2. William Russell Grace from Co. Laois was mayor of which American city known as 'The Big Apple'?

3. What football player from Ferrybank, Co. Waterford, has played for Manchester United and Sunderland and has been Captain of the Republic of Ireland team?

4. What type of food is celebrated with a festival in Kilmore Quay? a) seafood b) Italian food c) vegan food.

5. What is the Irish word for pig?

6. Leo Burdock's in Dublin is the oldest what in Ireland? a) pub b) chipper c) hotel.

7. In what Ulster county is the Uilleann Pipe Festival held every year?

8. What famous heavyweight boxer was made Freeman of Ennis?

9. What medicine was invented by Sir James Murray in Derry in 1817? Hint: You might take it for an upset stomach!

10. What county is home to Strangford Lough?

Round 4

1. What is the largest island in Lough Erne, Co. Fermanagh? a) Viper Island b) Cobra Island c) Boa Island.

2. In which county did Alcock and Brown land after the world's first transatlantic flight?

3. What kind of gardens would you find on the Irish National Stud farm in Kildare? a) French gardens b) American gardens c) Japanese gardens.

4. What mountains, found in Co. Laois, are one of the oldest mountain ranges in Europe? Slieve _____ Mountains.

5. Richard Harris, born in Limerick, is known for playing what famous wizard on film?

6. Old Mellifont Abbey, Ireland's first Cistercian monastery, can be found in which county?

7. Name one sport that would have been played at the Tailteann games, the ancient pre-Olympic Irish games.

8. There is a festival in Roscommon every year celebrating what type of meat?

9. What town in Tipperary is the birthplace of the Gaelic Athletic Association?

10. What Waterford cyclist was the World Number One for six years? ___ Kelly.

Round 5

1. How many counties beginning with 'W' are there in Ireland?

2. The Great Sugarloaf mountain is found in what county?

3. What is the Irish word for deer?

4. What date is 'Little Christmas', when the decorations are taken down?

5. Who is the song 'Cockles and Mussels' about?

6. In what county would you find the Newry Canal?

7. What is the name of the dramatic limestone landscape found in Co. Clare? The B____.

8. The Mussenden Temple is the symbol of what county in Ulster?

9. What sport is Eddie Irvine, born in Co. Down, famous for?

10. Enniskillen is a town in what county in Ulster?

Quiz

8

Round 1

1. Spiddal is the setting for what TV soap on TG4? *Ros na* ___.

2. Which female saint founded a double monastery in Kildare?

3. There is a festival in Portarlington every July celebrating what European nationality?

4. *Cill Chainnigh* is the Irish for what county?

5. St Peter's Church in Drogheda is famous for housing the preserved head of what Irish saint? Oliver P_____.

6. The comedian Tommy Tiernan is from what county?

7. Juan MacKenna was a war hero in what South American country? Hint: You might want to bring a jumper!

8. Which county in Connacht has the longest life expectancy in Ireland?

9. What influential folk band, popular in the 1960s, came from Tipperary? The C___ Brothers.

10. Robert Boyle, from Waterford, is known as the father of modern: a) physics b) chemistry c) biology.

Round 2

1. What type of birds come to the south-east of Wexford each winter? a) swallows b) geese c) swans.

2. What is the Irish word for potatoes?

3. What type of food is dulse, often eaten in Co. Antrim? Hint: It might be a bit salty!

4. In what county might you hear the phrase 'That's a pink horse of a different colour'?

5. Willie Clancy was famous for playing what instrument? a) uilleann pipes b) bagpipes c) fiddle.

6. Spell 'Portlaoise'.

7. True or false: Killyleagh Castle is the oldest occupied castle in Ireland.

8. In which county in Ulster would you find Lough Erne?

9. The round tower in Ardmore, Co. Waterford, was built by what saint?

10. The comedy film festival in Waterville is named after C____ Chaplin.

Round 3

1. What is the only doubly land-locked county in Ireland?

2. Lough Gur is home to the largest what in Ireland? a) castle b) passage tomb c) stone circle.

3. What well-known castle in Leinster was built for William Marshal, the 4th Earl of Pembroke?

4. Oweynagat in Roscommon means 'Cave of the C___'.

5. Carlingford in Louth has a festival every August celebrating what type of seafood?

6. In which county would you find the megalithic passage tombs at Newgrange?

7. What type of dairy food is Cashel Blue?

8. Arthur Leared from Wexford invented a type of: a) stethoscope b) x-ray c) thermometer.

9. *Madra rua* is Irish for what sly mammal?

10. What Hollywood actor, known for his roles in *Taken* and *Michael Collins*, comes from Ballymena in Co. Antrim?

Round 4

1. What rock and roll icon had ancestors in Hacketstown, Co. Carlow?

2. What county has won the Ulster Senior Football Championship more times than any other?

3. Middleton in Co. Cork is known for distilling what type of alcoholic drink? a) whiskey b) gin c) vodka.

4. How many counties in total are there in Ireland?

5. Arranmore is an island found off the coast of which county in Ulster?

6. Kippure is the highest mountain in Co. Dublin and the source of which river?

7. What type of egg laid in Tuam, Co. Galway, was the heaviest of its kind?

8. *An Lú* is the Irish for what county?

9. Eddie Macken competed in the Olympics in what sport?

10. Which television and radio presenter, best known for his work with the BBC, was born in Limerick? Terry W___.

Round 5

1. Ireland's biggest film studio, Ardmore Studios, are found in what county?

2. Mullaghmeen in Co. Westmeath has the largest forest of what type of tree in Ireland? a) beech b) oak c) sycamore.

3. In which county would you find the longest street in Northern Ireland?

4. True or false: storm petrels, choughs and black-throated divers are all types of fish.

5. Monaghan has one of the largest producers in the world of what natural food?

6. What film starring John Wayne was partly filmed in Cong, Co. Mayo? *The ____ Man*.

7. In which Leinster county would you find the Cooley Mountains?

8. What does the Irish word *oileán* mean?

9. The Irish Fly Fishing and Game Shooting museum is in which town in Laois?

10. Peig Sayers, author of *Peig*, came from what islands off the coast of Kerry? B____ Islands.

Quiz

9

Round 1

1. Lambay Island is found off the coast of what county in Leinster?

2. Sir Walter Raleigh is famous for planting what vegetable in Ireland?

3. A yellowhammer is: a) a plant b) a tool c) a bird.

4. Belfast City Airport is named after which famous footballer? George ____.

5. *Uachtar reoite* is the Irish for what cold dessert?

6. Name the activity park found in the Vale of Clara, Co. Wicklow.

7. In the story *The Children of Lir*, Lir's wife Aoife cursed his children to live as what for 300 years?

8. What is the biggest county in Northern Ireland?

9. What famous Irish poet spent his childhood holidays in Sligo and wrote many poems about the county? ____ ____ Yeats.

10. Lifford is a town in which Ulster county?

Round 2

1. Beech, spruce and ash are all types of what?

2. Sir Francis Beaufort was born in Navan and created the Beaufort Scale, which is used to measure: a) rain b) wind c) earthquakes.

3. In what county in Leinster would you find the most richly decorated High Cross in Ireland?

4. *Port Láirge* is the Irish for which county?

5. What islands off the coast of Kerry are home to many varieties of bird, including puffins? S_____ Islands.

6. A Galway Hooker, which has its own festival in Kinvara every year, is a type of: a) bird b) boat c) cow.

7. Which football club plays their home games in Tallaght Stadium? _____ Rovers.

8. What Irish folk and country singer grew up in Kincasslagh, Co. Donegal? _____ O'Donnell.

9. What town in Cork was the last port of call for the *Titanic*? C___.

10. The Galtee Mountains are found in which two Munster counties?

Round 3

1. What famous TV show about priests was filmed in Co. Clare?

2. In which county beginning with 'C' would you find the Brownshill Dolmen, with the largest capstone in Europe?

3. A pollan is a type of: a) fish b) tree c) butterfly.

4. *Teach solais* is the Irish for what life-saving building?

5. Yola is an extinct dialect of English once spoken in which Leinster county?

6. Gallybander is Waterford slang for: a) a hurley b) a slingshot c) a fork.

7. What actor and comedian from Tipperary is known for starring in *Killinaskully*? Pat _____.

8. What berries are often eaten at Bellewstown racecourse in Co Meath?

9. What former Irish president was born in Co. Mayo? Mary _____.

10. True or false: Friesian cows are raised mainly for their meat.

Round 4

1. In which county beginning with 'L' would you find Ardee Castle?

2. Thomas Fitzgerald from Limerick was the great grandfather of which US president? John F. _____.

3. What was Dame Alice Kyteler accused of being, which caused her to flee Ireland? a) a mermaid b) a banshee c) a witch.

4. In which Munster county would you find Blennerville Windmill, the tallest tower mill in Europe?

5. Who visited Galway fifteen years before he discovered America?

6. What Dublin town was founded by St Colmcille? S____.

7. If someone from Donegal mentioned their 'aul doll', who would they be talking about?

8. What type of precious metal is mined in the Sperrin Mountains?

9. In what county would you find The Burren?

10. How many counties in Ireland begin with 'K'?

Round 5

1. *Ceatharlach* is the Irish for what county?

2. In what county would you find Coolmore Stud, the world's largest breeder of racehorses?

3. On December 26th, who goes around houses collecting money for a party in their town? ___ boys.

4. *Deilf* is the Irish for what aquatic mammal?

5. What is the oldest operating lighthouse in the world, found in Co. Wexford? H___ Head.

6. What county in Munster is known as the 'Crystal County'?

7. What Meath town has a palindromic placename (one that is spelled the same backwards and forwards)?

8. Longford has all the native Irish species of what flying insect?

9. Because the land in Co. Leitrim is so wet, people joke that it is sold by the g_____ rather than by the acre.

10. In which county would you find the oldest steam rally in Ireland?

Quiz

10

Round 1

1. True or false: Gowran in Co. Kilkenny has Ireland's only reptile zoo.

2. What mountain range is home to Carrauntoohil, the highest peak in Ireland? M_____Reeks.

3. *Luimneach* is the Irish for what county?

4. The wheel of which saint is the symbol of Tuam, Co. Galway? St J____.

5. John M. Synge wrote the play *The Playboy of the W_____ W_____.*

6. In which county in Ulster would you find Dundonald Leisure Park, home to an Olympic-sized ice rink?

7. Dana was Ireland's first winner of what song competition?

8. The English Market is a food market found in what city?

9. What is Ireland's longest river?

10. Constance Markievicz, the nationalist, suffragette and socialist, grew up in what county in Connacht?

Round 2

1. In what Munster county would you find Cahir Castle, which looks like it is growing from the rock it sits on?

2. How many counties in Ireland begin with 'T'?

3. What colours are on the Irish tricolour?

4. The author Eoin Colfer from Co. Wexford is best known for writing what science fiction series? *Artemis* ____.

5. *Cláirseach* is the Irish for what stringed instrument?

6. Corca Dhuibhne and Uíbh Ráthach are two Gaeltachts in which county?

7. The shortest St Patrick's Day parade in the world takes place in the village of Dripsey in what county?

8. What county in Ulster is known as the Lakeland County?

9. In which county would you find Lough Corrib?

10. Name the biscuit that has pink marshmallow and jam on top.

Round 3

1. Who was the Antarctic explorer from Annascaul, Co. Kerry, known as the Irish Giant? Tom ____.

2. Co. Wexford is known for its flavoursome variety of what kind of fruit?

3. Henry Shefflin from Ballyhale, Co. Kilkenny, is known for playing which sport?

4. In what county would you find the smallest chapel in Ireland?

5. Aughnacliffe in Co. Longford means 'The Field of the _____': a) dogs b) stones c) bones.

6. Manorhamilton is a town in what county?

7. A red hand is the emblem of what GAA team?

8. In which county in Connacht would you find the Yeats Memorial Building?

9. Ernest Walton won a Nobel Prize for: a) splitting the atom b) solving world hunger c) inventing antibiotics.

10. What famous myth about children who are turned into swans took place on Lough Derravaragh, Co. Westmeath?

Round 4

1. Mutton Island is found off the coast of which county in Munster?

2. Name the Cork-born footballer who has played for both Manchester United and the Republic of Ireland: Roy ____.

3. Derry is nicknamed the ___ Leaf County.

4. In what county is the Twelve Bens mountain range?

5. The bones of what animal were found in Poll na mBéar in Co. Leitrim?

6. Who was the first female president of Ireland?

7. What county has won more Hurling All-Irelands than any other county?

8. Billy Roll is a type of: a) ham b) dance c) cake.

9. How many counties in Ireland begin with the letter 'L'?

10. What city in Munster is known as the oldest city in Ireland?

Round 5

1. In what Leinster county would you find Belvedere House?

2. *Cnónna* is Irish for what crunchy snack?

3. In which Ulster county would you find the Bluestack Mountains?

4. Which of the following is **NOT** a type of lemonade sold in Ireland? a) red lemonade b) purple lemonade c) brown lemonade.

5. Bunratty Castle is in what county?

6. What type of foreign coins were found in Cloghan, Co. Offaly? a) Roman coins b) Greek coins c) Turkish coins.

7. What is the name of the only wildlife park in Ireland, found in Cork?

8. Spell 'barmbrack'.

9. In which county would you find Jerpoint Abbey?

10. Which island is the only place in Ireland to still have its own king? T___ Island.

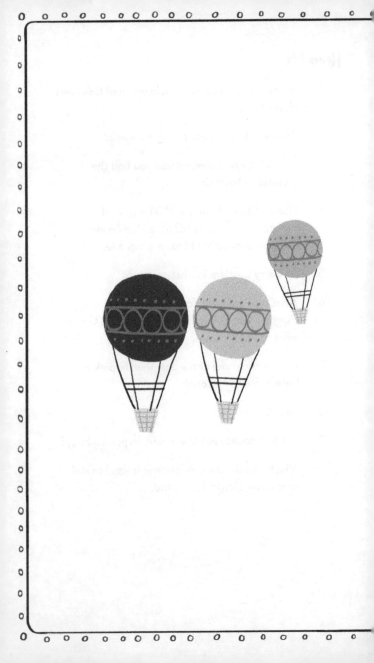

ANSWERS

Quiz

1

Round 1

1. What county beginning with 'M' is known as the drumlin county?
   Monaghan

2. The Nobel Prize-winning poet Seamus _____ attended St Columb's college in Co. Derry.
   Heaney

3. Yellowman, sold in Co. Antrim, is a type of:
   a) footwear b) sweet c) garden tool.
   c) sweet

4. *Seilide* is the Irish for what slimy-shelled creature?
   Snail

5. Poc Fada is a long-distance style of what GAA sport?
   Hurling

6. What is the capital of the Republic of Ireland?
   Dublin

7. The remains of which romantic saint are buried in Whitefriar Street Church in Dublin?
   St Valentine

8. What province is Co. Wicklow in?
   Leinster

9. What mythical couple are said to be buried at Benbulbin in Co. Sligo?
   Diarmuid and Gráinne

10. The most northerly point in Ireland is called _____ Head.
    Malin

Round 2

1. In Co. Mayo, there is a National Museum of
   _____ Life.
   Country

2. What floating mode of transportation once
   crashed into the town of Tullamore?
   Hot air balloon

3. Spell 'Laois', the county in Leinster.
   Laois

4. James Martin, born in Co. Down, invented the:
   a) ejection seat b) telescope c) cornflake.
   a) ejection seat

5. John B. Keane, from Co. Kerry, wrote a play
   called *The* _____, about two men fighting over
   farmland.
   The Field

6. There is a festival in Longford town every
   September celebrating what stringed instrument?
   Banjo

7. On what date do people from the country
   traditionally travel to Dublin to do their
   Christmas shopping?
   December 8th

8. James Farrell from Co. Longford saved the lives
   of two girls on what famous sinking ship?
   Titanic

9. What comedian and television host, known for hosting *Mock the Week*, was born in Bray, Co. Wicklow: D____ O'B_____.
   Dara O'Briain

10. The king of Ireland was crowned on what hill in Co. Meath? Hint: It's also a woman's name!
    Hill of Tara

Round 3

1. What type of sweaters are special to the Galway area?
    Aran sweaters

2. The penalty kick was invented by: a) George Best b) William McCrum c) Lionel Messi.
    b) William McCrum

3. There is a museum and heritage centre in Limerick dedicated to former President and Taoiseach, Éamon ___ ___.
    Éamon de Valera

4. Monasterevin in Co. Kildare is also known as 'The ___ of Ireland' because it has many bridges, just like the city in Italy.
    Venice

5. What is said to be buried under the Rock of Dunamase in Laois? Hint: Pirates are known for burying this!
    Treasure

6. In Fermanagh, there is a meaty delicacy known as Black ___.
    Bacon

7. Coumshingaun in Co. Waterford is a fine example of a type of what?
    Corrie lake

8. What is the Irish word for milk?
    Bainne

9.   The only two Gaeltacht areas in Leinster, Baile
     Ghib and Ráth Cairn, are found in which county?
     Co. Meath

10. What famous golfer comes from Holywood in Co.
     Down?
     Rory McIlroy

Round 4

1. Name the only county in Ireland beginning with 'R'.
   Roscommon

2. Bulmers, which comes from Clonmel in Tipperary, is a type of: a) cider b) cola c) whiskey.
   Cider

3. Name the singer-songwriter born in Co. Dublin, best known for her song 'Nothing Compares 2 U': _____ O'Connor.
   Sinead O'Connor

4. In what Leinster county would you find the town of Muine Bheag?
   Carlow

5. What Irish sporting organisation was founded by Michael Cusack?
   The GAA

6. Pilgrims travel to what town in Co. Mayo to honour the Virgin Mary?
   Knock

7. In which county in Connacht would you find Carrowmore, the biggest megalithic site in Ireland?
   Co. Sligo

8. John Joe Nevin, born in Mullingar, is known for what Olympic sport?
   Boxing

9. Rissoles, sold in chippers in Wexford, are a type of fried: a) chocolate bar b) potato cake c) sausage.
   b) potato cake

10. Lugnaquilla is the highest point in which mountain range: W_____ Mountains?
    Wicklow Mountains

Round 5

1. What Olympic medal-winning female runner was
    born in Cobh, Co. Cork?
    Sonia O'Sullivan

2. Mount Brandon in Co. Kerry is a popular spot for:
    a) golfers b) bird watchers c) pilgrims.
    c) pilgrims

3. Margaret Haughery is known for opening what in
    New Orleans to help children?
    Orphanages

4. In which county would you find Loftus Hall, one
    of the most haunted places in Ireland?
    Co. Wexford

5. Who wrote the novel *Gulliver's Travels*?
    Jonathan ____.
    Jonathan Swift

6. What fizzy drink do Irish people drink flat when
    they're sick?
    7Up

7. The Bridge of Tears in Limerick was a famous
    place to say goodbye when people were
    emigrating to where?
    North America

8. Spell 'dolmen', a type of megalithic tomb.
    Dolmen

9. What city in Antrim is musician Van Morrison from?
    Belfast

10. What mythological Irish hero is said to have tied himself to a standing stone at Knockbridge as he was dying? C_____.
    Cúchulainn

Quiz 2

Round 1

1. What Munster county was the GAA started in?
   Tipperary

2. What type of buzzing insects would you find in an apiary?
   Bees

3. *Camán* is the Irish for what piece of sporting equipment?
   Hurley

4. What well-known crisps are made in Tandragee in Co. Armagh?
   Tayto

5. The Lambert Puppet Theatre in Monkstown made a children's TV series about which red-haired puppet?
   Bosco

6. Which of the following was **NOT** found in the Bog of Allen: a) a canoe b) a jewellery box c) butter.
   b) a jewellery box

7. There is a festival in Granard celebrating what stringed musical instrument which is also found on Irish money?
   The harp

8. Which park is home to Dublin Zoo?
   Phoenix Park

9. A goosander is: a) a fish b) a duck c) an insect.
   b) a duck

10. People from which county are nicknamed 'The Cats'?
    Kilkenny

Round 2

1. A type of polo was invented in Wicklow where the players ride on what instead of horses?
   Bicycle

2. Carrickmacross is well known for making what type of pretty fabric?
   Lace

3. What football player, born in Rathfarnham, has played for Newcastle United, Chelsea, Fulham, Blackburn Rovers and the Republic of Ireland?
   Damien Duff

4. What Ulster county has the slogan 'Up here it's different'?
   Co. Donegal

5. What do you call the floury bread bun eaten in Waterford?
   Blaa

6. In which county might you be able to attend a Pork Festival and witness the *Olympigs*?
   Co. Cavan

7. What famous landmark in Co. Antrim is made of 40,000 rock columns?
   The Giant's Causeway

8. In Lough Ree there have been sightings of:
   a) a monster b) a mermaid c) a whale.
   a) a monster

9. What is the Irish word for bread
   Arán

10. The owner of The King's Head pub in Galway once did an unpleasant task for Oliver Cromwell. What did he do?
    He cut off a king's head

Round 3

1. In what county beginning with 'W' would you find
    the longest handmade stone bridge in Ireland?
    Wicklow

2. What town in Mayo was voted the best place
    to live in Ireland and has won the Tidy Towns
    competition many times? W_____.
    Westport

3. What province is Waterford in?
    Munster

4. What is the name of the Dublin-born mixed
    martial artist and UFC champion?
    Conor McGregor

5. What type of fruit is a Bramley's Seedling?
    Apple

6. Belfast-born writer C. S. Lewis wrote *The
    Chronicles of* ____.
    Narnia

7. What animal is Tipperary famous for breeding?
    Horses

8. Which waterfall rises in the Devil's Punchbowl in
    Co. Kerry? T___ Waterfall.
    Torc

9. Who shows up to weddings in the West wearing
    straw masks?
    Strawboys

10. What should you kiss to receive the 'Gift of the Gab'?
    The Blarney Stone

Round 4

1. What is the only county with a 'V' in its name?
    Cavan

2. What popular music festival takes place in
    Stradbally Estate in Laois every summer?
    Electric Picnic

3. In what county would you find Mullyash Mountain?
    Monaghan

4. Football Special is a type of: a) TV show b) fizzy
    drink c) sports shop.
    b) fizzy drink

5. The ancestors of what famous mouse-loving
    animator are buried in Ballyloo, Co. Carlow?
    Walt Disney

6. Glendalough is in what county?
    Wicklow

7. Spell 'Tipperary'.
    Tipperary

8. Which island is the biggest of the Aran Islands?
    a) Inis Mór b) Inis Meáin c) Inis Oírr
    a) Inis Mór

9. How many provinces are there in Ireland?
    Four

10. Which famous festival for Irish women around the
    world is celebrated in Tralee every year?
    Rose of Tralee

Round 5

1. What type of dog was Fury, who saved the life of a child in Portumna castle?
   Irish wolfhound

2. Joe Dolan was a pop singer from what county?
   Westmeath

3. What water sport is very popular in Bundoran, Co. Donegal?
   Surfing

4. What famous Irish saint worked as a shepherd on Slemish Mountain?
   St Patrick

5. What is the name of the stadium in Dublin where Ireland's football and rugby home games are played?
   Aviva Stadium

6. The town of Castlebar is in what Connacht county?
   Mayo

7. A kittiwake is a type of: a) flower b) rodent c) bird.
   c) bird

8. The Dunbrody Famine Ship is found in which county?
   Co. Wexford

9. It is said that the Rock of Cashel was made when Satan took a bite out of a mountain and spat it away. What was the name of the mountain? D____ B__ Mountain.
   Devil's Bit Mountain

10. Meath is Ireland's leading producer of what crop? Hint: It's very popular with Mr Tayto!
    Potatoes

Quiz
3

Round 1

1. Which city in Ulster is the most complete walled city in Europe?
    Derry

2. What famous Irish writer is known for his books *Ulysses*, *Dubliners* and *Finnegans Wake*? J____ J____.
    James Joyce

3. In what county would you find Reginald's Tower?
    Waterford

4. According to legend, a king in Loughmore Castle offered his daughter's hand in marriage in exchange for: a) killing a boar b) swimming to Wales c) baking a pie.
    a) killing a boar

5. Who was born in Callan, Co. Kilkenny, and was the founder of the Christian Brothers? Hint: His last name is a type of food! Edmund ___.
    Edmund Rice

6. What county is home to Aillwee Cave?
    Co. Clare

7. What famous song was written about the Athenry area?
    'The Fields of Athenry'

8. Turlough O'Carolan, who was blind, was famous for playing what instrument?
    Harp

9.   Tayto Park in Co. Meath is home to Ireland's first herd of what American animal?
     Bison/Buffalo

10. Oliver Goldsmith from Co. Longford made up what term, describing someone who always follows the rules and does everything right?
     Goody two-shoes

Round 2

1. The city of Newry is split between what two counties? A___ and D__.
   Armagh and Down

2. A yew is a type of: a) drink b) tree c) boat.
   b) tree

3. There is a competition in Freshford, Co. Kilkenny, called the Irish C____ Championships. Hint: You need some horse chestnuts to take part!
   Irish Conker Championships

4. What Waterford company was the very first maker of cream crackers?
   Jacob's

5. The devil is said to have visited Loftus Hall in Co. Wexford. What did he leave in the roof?
   A hole

6. In what city is a Jazz Festival held every October?
   Cork

7. What date is St Patrick's Day?
   March 17th

8. *Mála tae* is the Irish for what essential kitchen item?
   Tea bag

9. Which well-known poet comes from Monaghan? Patrick _____.
   Kavanagh

10. What is the name of Ireland's National GAA
    Stadium?
    Croke Park

Round 3

1. Andrea, Sharon, Caroline and Jim are siblings in what famous family music act from Louth?
   The Corrs

2. In what county would you find the Mermaid Stones of Scurmore?
   Co. Sligo

3. How many counties in Ireland start with 'C'?
   Four

4. The first Irish tricolour flag was raised in what county?
   Waterford

5. Phil Lynott was the frontman of which Dublin band? Hint: Skinny Elizabeth!
   Thin Lizzy

6. What is the name of W. B. Yeats' brother, who was a famous artist?
   Jack Butler Yeats

7. The ferry service in Rosslare brings people to what two countries?
   Wales and France

8. *Colúr* is Irish for what type of city-living bird?
   Pigeon

9. What is Ireland's main centre for water sports, found in Co. Dublin? National _____ Centre.
   National Aquatic Centre

10. The River Shannon begins in which county?
    Co. Cavan

Round 4

1. Lilliput House in Co. Westmeath was used by which author as a holiday home? Jonathan ____.
   Jonathan Swift

2. A gillaroo is a type of: a) trout b) rabbit c) lizard.
   a) trout

3. What guitarist and songwriter is remembered with a statue in his hometown of Ballyshannon? Rory G____.
   Rory Gallagher

4. The city of Belfast is mostly in what county?
   Co. Antrim

5. Puck Fair in Killorglan crowns a mountain ____ as king of the town every year.
   Goat

6. New Ross is in what county?
   Wexford

7. What type of dog is Mick the Miller, who has his own statue in Offaly?
   Greyhound

8. Darren Clarke from Dungannon in Tyrone is a professional in what sport?
   Golf

9. In which county would you find Tullynally castle?
   Westmeath

10. What is the biggest town in Donegal? L_____y.
Letterkenny

Round 5

1. Which county in Ulster is Ireland's second biggest producer of crystal?
   Co. Cavan

2. Physicist John Tyndall is famous for explaining:
   a) why the sky is blue b) why birds can fly c) why grass is green.
   a) why the sky is blue

3. The town of Tullamore is in what county in Leinster?
   Offaly

4. What bumpy skin infection is St Patrick's Well in Tyrone supposed to be good at healing?
   Warts

5. True or false: Cupidstown Hill is the highest point in Kildare.
   True

6. In which county was Michael D. Higgins born?
   Limerick

7. What meat product, usually eaten at breakfast, was developed in Waterford by Henry Denny in 1820?
   Rashers

8. What TV show do Irish people stay up to watch and find out about the latest toys for Christmas?
   The Late Late Toy Show

9. Carnagh East is a town in the very centre of
   Ireland – what county is it in?
   Roscommon

10. Spell 'Fermanagh'.
    Fermanagh

Quiz

4

Round 1

1. Which Gaelic games commentator comes from Dún Síon in Co. Kerry? _____ Ó Muircheartaigh.
   Mícheál Ó Muircheartigh

2. Former US presidents Ulysses S. Grant and Woodrow Wilson had ancestors from what Irish county?
   Co. Tyrone

3. What breed of dog hails from Kerry and is used for hunting and guarding your home? Kerry _____ Terrier.
   Kerry Blue Terrier

4. What is the name of the comedy festival that takes place annually in Kilkenny?
   The Cat Laughs Festival

5. How many counties beginning with 'A' are there in Ireland?
   Two

6. Oliver Goldsmith is a novelist and playwright from which county in Leinster?
   Longford

7. A traditional music festival held in Monaghan every May has a competition for players of what stringed instrument?
   Fiddle

8. What is the highest hill in Co. Westmeath, but the lowest county top in the country?
   Mullaghmeen

9. Glencar Waterfall in Co. Leitrim was mentioned in a poem by what Irish poet? W. B. ____.
   W. B. Yeats

10. 'Poke' is a word used in Co. Down for what type of sweet treat, often eaten by the seaside?
    Ice cream cones

Round 2

1. Which county in Ireland has the shortest coastline?
   Leitrim

2. Neil Jordan from Co. Sligo directed what film about a famous Irish nationalist leader? M_____ C_____.
   Michael Collins

3. On a clear day, what country can you see from the top of the Great Sugarloaf?
   Wales

4. Shellakybooky is a Waterford name for what slimy, shelled animal?
   A snail

5. The grounds of what castle in Co. Meath have been used to host rock concerts since 1981?
   Slane Castle

6. A Little Tern is: a) a frog b) a bird c) a cake.
   b) a bird

7. Which river runs through Galway city? River C___.
   River Corrib

8. In what county in Ulster is Belleek Pottery made?
   Co. Fermanagh

9. Christy Moore wrote a song about a town that also holds a matchmaking event every year. Name the town.

   Lisdoonvarna

10. What famous ship was built in the Harland and Wolff shipyard in Belfast?

    Titanic

Round 3

1. Who is the lead singer of the Dublin band U2?
   Bono

2. *Éala* is the Irish word for what graceful bird?
   Swan

3. How many counties are there in Ulster?
   Nine

4. Michael Davitt, who started the National Land League, was from which county?
   Mayo

5. When the waters of Lough Allen are low, you can see: a) treasure b) crannogs c) eels.
   b) crannogs

6. Marble Arch was home to what extinct giant animal? Hint: It was much bigger than Bambi!
   Giant Irish Deer/Elk

7. What do Dubliners call the Natural History Museum? The ___ Zoo.
   The Dead Zoo

8. According to legend, who built the Giant's Causeway?
   Fionn mac Cumhaill

9. Armagh is the only city in the world with two cathedrals of the same name. They are both called St _____.
   St Patrick's

10. Mondello Park is Ireland's only international
    venue for what sport?
    Motorsport

Round 4

1. In what county would you find Croagh Patrick, where many people go on pilgrimages?
   Mayo

2. Falmouth Kearney from Moneygall was the great-great-great grandfather of which US president?
   Barack Obama

3. What apple-flavoured fizzy drink was first made in Clonmel, Co. Tipperary?
   Cidona

4. What is the longest river in Ireland?
   River Shannon

5. The hibernation den of the brown ____ can be found in Aillwee Cave.
   Bear

6. What Irish city in Ulster is also known as Stroke City?
   Derry

7. Rev. James McDonald was an ancestor of Rudyard Kipling, who wrote a book about Mowgli and Baloo the bear. Name the book.
   The Jungle Book

8. What sport takes place in Punchestown racecourse?
   Horse racing

9. Name the ninth president of Ireland, born in Limerick, who is also a poet, sociologist and author.
    Michael D. Higgins

10. What world-famous brooch was found on a beach in Bettystown?
    Tara Brooch

Round 5

1. Mullingar is a town in what Leinster county?
   Westmeath

2. What is the Irish word for cheese?
   Cáis

3. Peter O'Toole, born in Connemara, starred in the film *Lawrence of* _____?
   Lawrence of Arabia

4. In which county was Ireland's first Lifeboat Station set up?
   Co. Dublin

5. How many Gaeltacht areas are there in Co. Cork?
   Two

6. John Philip Holland from Co. Clare is known for inventing: a) the hot air balloon b) the kayak c) the submarine.
   c) the submarine

7. What boxing champion comes from Bray, Co. Wicklow?
   Katie Taylor

8. In which city is the book *Angela's Ashes* by Frank McCourt set?
   Limerick

9. What castle in Kildare was built in the 13th century as home to the FitzGerald family?
Maynooth Castle

10. The Ox Mountains are found in which county?
Co. Sligo

Quiz
5

Round 1

1. Charles Stewart _____ was born in Rathdrum, Co. Wicklow, and has a memorial park dedicated to him.
   Parnell

2. How many bridges are there in Cork city? a) 38 b) 29 c) 16.
   b) 29

3. What is Ireland's most visited natural attraction? Hint: You have to keep away from the edge!
   Cliffs of Moher

4. How many counties are there in Munster?
   Six

5. Which of these is **NOT** a type of duck? a) wigeon b) indigo c) teal.
   b) indigo

6. Athenry is a town in what county?
   Co. Galway

7. What can you find in Birr, Co. Offaly, that you can use to look at the stars?
   A telescope

8. What boyband singer comes from Mullingar, Co. Westmeath?
   Niall Horan

9. What date is St Brigid's Day?
   February 1st

10. The Slieve Aughty mountains spread from Galway into what county?

      Clare

Round 2

1. Torpey is the leading brand of what piece of GAA equipment?
    Hurleys

2. What hot drink was invented by Sir Hans Sloane from Killyleagh?
    Hot chocolate

3. In what county would you find St Mel's Cathedral?
    Longford

4. How many counties in Ireland start with 'D'?
    Four

5. The Céide Fields in Co. Mayo are the remains of a farming community from the ____ Age.
    Stone Age

6. What seafood is celebrated with a festival in Clarenbridge, Co. Galway?
    Oysters

7. The heart of St Laurence O'Toole can be found in ____ Church Cathedral.
    Christ Church Cathedral

8. What county's GAA team is nicknamed The Scallion Eaters?
    Carlow

9. What river runs through Cork city?
    River Lee

10. Which famous leader appeared on the Irish £20 note and has a street named after him in Dublin city? Daniel _____.
    Daniel O'Connell

Round 3

1. True or false: Visitors go to Newgrange on the summer solstice every year to see the inner chambers light up.
    False – they go on the winter solstice

2. What museum in Roscommon remembers a very hungry time in Irish history? Irish National F_____ Museum.
    Irish National Famine Museum

3. Brian Friel, the playwright born in Tyrone, wrote a play called _____ at Lughnasa?
    Dancing at Lughnasa

4. In what Leinster county would you find Powerscourt House, which has beautiful walled gardens?
    Wicklow

5. Which of these rivers does **NOT** flow through Kildare? a) River Barrow b) River Liffey c) River Lee.
    c) River Lee

6. Veda, a food popular in Northern Ireland, is a type of: a) bread b) meat pie c) creamy dessert.
    a) bread

7. Which airport has the longest runway in Ireland?
    Shannon Airport

8. In what county beginning with 'C' would you find over 360 lakes?
   Co. Cavan

9. What is the Irish word for bridge?
   Droichead

10. Ireland's first bottled mineral water was made in what county?
    Co. Tipperary

Round 4

1. What are crubeens made from?
   Pig's feet

2. Percy French wrote a song called 'Come Back Paddy Reilly to Ballyjamesduff' about: a) his brother b) his doctor c) his driver.
   c) his driver

3. Bushmills is known for what type of alcoholic drink?
   Whiskey

4. What famous female pilot landed just outside Derry city on her solo transatlantic flight? _____ Earheart.
   Amelia

5. How many counties are there in Leinster?
   Twelve

6. What festival celebrating something used to frighten birds is celebrated in Co. Laois?
   Scarecrow Festival

7. The Ardagh Chalice was found by two boys in: a) a river b) a football pitch c) a potato field.
   c) a potato field

8. What famous female saint is believed to have been born in Faughart, Co. Louth?
   St Brigid

9. Which of these is **NOT** a type of bird? a) crossbill
   b) guppy c) whimbrel.
   b) guppy

10. What castle in Co. Offaly is one of the most
    haunted castles in Ireland? L___ Castle.
    Leap Castle

Round 5

1. In what Leinster county would you find a haunted
    gaol?
      Wicklow

2. William Jacob started making what type of food
    in Waterford in 1851?
      Biscuits

3. What Sligo-born actress played the role of tea-
    loving Mrs Doyle in *Father Ted*? _____ McLynn.
      Pauline McLynn

4. What village in Limerick has been called Ireland's
    prettiest village?
      Adare

5. What dairy manufacturer has its headquarters on
    the edge of Kilkenny city? Hint: Its name in Irish
    means 'clean food'.
      Glanbia

6. Spell 'Monaghan'.
      Monaghan

7. Ken Doherty is a world professional champion in
    what sport?
      Snooker

8. The corkscrew-shaped barn found in Co. Kildare
    is called: a) The Brilliant Barn b) The Wonderful
    Barn c) The Pretty Great Barn.
      b) The Wonderful Barn

9. What is the home ground of Munster Rugby?
    Thomond Park

10. What is the name of the home of Lady Gregory,
    co-founder of the Abbey Theatre? C___ Park.
    Coole Park

Quiz
6

Round 1

1. Three members of which famous boyband were born in Sligo?
   Westlife

2. In what county might you hear a person say 'This is me, is that you?' when answering the phone?
   Co. Leitrim

3. The Lady of the Lake is a mythical figure found in: a) Lough Erne b) Lough Arrow c) Loch Ness.
   a) Lough Erne

4. What brand of crisps has its own theme park in Co. Meath?
   Tayto

5. Which canal goes from Dublin to Abbeyshrule in Longford?
   The Royal Canal

6. What famous cinematic lion was born in Dublin Zoo?
   The MGM Lion/Leo the Lion

7. In which county in Ulster could you attend Europe's biggest Bob Dylan music festival?
   Co. Donegal

8. What popular folk singer, known for songs such as 'Lisdoonvarna' and 'Don't Forget Your Shovel', is from Kildare? Christy ____.
   Christy Moore

9. Glen Lough Nature Reserve has a large number of what bird? Whooper ____.
   Whooper swans

10. Birr Castle Estate is home to the largest ____ in Ireland: a) see-saw b) maze c) tree house.
    c) tree house

Round 2

1. The water in St Feichin's Well, Co. Westmeath, is
   special because it will not _____?
   Boil

2. What Leinster county holds Ireland's longest-
   running air show?
   Co. Longford

3. What restaurant and cookery school in Co. Cork
   is famous for its yummy relish?
   Ballymaloe

4. What cosmic material landed in a potato field in
   Clonoulty in 1865?
   A meteorite

5. What unusual championships, which take place
   in Castleblayney, involve swimming in a trench?
   Irish B__ S_____ Championships.
   Irish Bog Snorkelling Championships

6. The Cliffs of Moher are found in which county?
   Co. Clare

7. What famous Irish king is said to be buried in
   Armagh? B___ B__.
   Brian Boru

8. Clouded yellow, red admiral and painted lady are
   all types of what fluttering insect?
   Butterfly

9. In which Connacht county could you play a tune on the Musical Bridge?
   Co. Mayo

10. A bonham is a young: a) pig b) sheep c) duck.
    a) pig

Round 3

1. What is the name of the official home of the President of Ireland?
   Áras an Uachtaráin

2. How many counties are there in Connacht?
   Five

3. The Marble Arch Caves are in counties Cavan and _____?
   Fermanagh

4. Which famous nationalist leader was from Clonakilty in Co. Cork? Michael _____.
   Michael Collins

5. What seafood is celebrated with a festival on Valentia Island? a) scallops b) prawns c) scampi.
   a) scallops

6. Architect James Hoban designed which famous building in Washington DC?
   The White House

7. In what town would you find Co. Cork's only horse-racing course?
   Mallow

8. In which county would you find the Dartry Mountains?
   Co. Leitrim

9. What town in Mayo has its own airport?
   Knock

10. Carlingford is a town in what Leinster county?
    Co. Louth

Round 4

1. What mountain is considered the holiest in Ireland? Croagh ____.
   Croagh Patrick

2. Ardal O'Hanlon from Monaghan played which simple-minded character in the TV show Father Ted?
   Dougal McGuire

3. Roscommon is Ireland's biggest producer of what meat?
   Lamb

4. Laurence Sterne, author of *The Life and Opinions of Tristram Shandy, Gentleman*, is from what county beginning with 'T'?
   Co. Tipperary

5. 'Red Lead' is another name for what type of sandwich meat?
   Luncheon sausage

6. There is an arboretum in Co. Wexford named after US president John F. Kennedy. What would you find in an arboretum?
   Trees

7. What is the Irish word for sausages?
   Ispíní

8. What is the capital city of Northern Ireland?
   Belfast

9. True or false: Pierce Butler from Co. Carlow signed the American Constitution.
   True

10. In what Munster county would you find Loop Head?
    Co. Clare

Round 5

1. What mountain range is found in Derry? a) Slieve
    Bernagh Mountains b) Slieve Bloom Mountains
    c) Sperrin Mountains.
    c) Sperrin Mountains

2. What important farming vehicle was invented by
    Harry Ferguson of Co. Down?
    The tractor

3. Fionn mac Cumhaill's Irish wolfhounds were said
    to be turned into what by a witch? a) mountains
    b) rabbits c) hurleys.
    a) mountains

4. What famous aquatic mammal lives in Dingle, Co.
    Kerry?
    Fungie the dolphin

5. Naas is the county town of what county?
    Co. Kildare

6. What female chef and food writer was born in
    Cullohill, Co. Laois? Darina ____.
    Darina Allen

7. The Hunt Museum in Limerick city contains art
    by what famous Spanish modern artist? Pablo

    ____.
    Pablo Picasso

8. Dermot O'Brien was a musician who also played
    what sport?
    Gaelic football

9. Name the famous passage tomb found in Co. Meath.
   Newgrange

10. In which Leinster county would you find the Irish Parachute Club?
    Co. Offaly

Quiz

7

Round 1

1. Chris O'Dowd from Co. Roscommon stars in the comedy TV show _____ Boy.
   Moone Boy

2. Mullaghmore is one of the best locations in the world for what water sport?
   Surfing

3. Castlederg, Co. Tyrone, hosts a fair every year for what type of fruit?
   Apple

4. Sean's Bar in Athlone is famous for being:
   a) the smallest pub in Ireland b) the oldest pub in Europe c) the cheapest pub in the world.
   b) the oldest pub in Europe

5. Eddie Jordan, who grew up in Bray, is known for what sport?
   Formula One

6. What vegetable was traditionally used in Ireland for carving faces on Halloween?
   A turnip

7. *Sútha talún* is the Irish for what sweet berries?
   Strawberries

8. What is the name of the river that runs through Dublin city?
   River Liffey

9. What county in Ulster is also known as 'The Orchard County'?
   Co. Armagh

10. What kind of animal is the goldeneye? a) bird b) dog c) fish
    a) bird

Round 2

1. In which county in Munster would you find the holiday village of Trabolgan?
   Co. Cork

2. True or false: Killybegs is the smallest fishing port in Ireland.
   False – it's the largest!

3. What Dalkey-born author wrote *Circle of Friends* and *Tara Road*? Maeve B____.
   Maeve Binchy

4. What breed of pony, bred in Galway, has its own show every August?
   Connemara Pony

5. Which county does Newbridge Silverware come from?
   Co. Kildare

6. Frank McCourt, born in Limerick, wrote what book based on his childhood? *Angela's A____.*
   Angela's Ashes

7. Spell 'Connacht'.
   Connacht

8. What famous actor, known for his role as James Bond, grew up in Navan? ____ Brosnan.
   Pierce Brosnan

9. Brian O'Nolan, the novelist and playwright, wrote under what name? F___ O'Brien.
   Flann O'Brien

10. 'Well that beats Banagher!' is a phrase referring to a town in which county?
    Co. Offaly

Round 3

1. The Lily Lolly Craftfest in Sligo celebrates Susan and Elizabeth, sisters of which famous Irish poet? W. B. ____.
   W. B. Yeats

2. William Russell Grace from Co. Laois was mayor of which American city known as 'The Big Apple'?
   New York

3. What football player from Ferrybank, Co. Waterford, has played for Manchester United and Sunderland and has been Captain of the Republic of Ireland team?
   John O'Shea

4. What type of food is celebrated with a festival in Kilmore Quay? a) seafood b) Italian food c) vegan food.
   a) seafood

5. What is the Irish word for pig?
   Muc

6. Leo Burdock's in Dublin is the oldest what in Ireland? a) pub b) chipper c) hotel.
   b) chipper

7. In what Ulster county is the Uilleann Pipe Festival held every year?
   Co. Armagh

8. What famous heavyweight boxer was made Freeman of Ennis?
   Muhammad Ali

9. What medicine was invented by Sir James Murray in Derry in 1817? Hint: You might take it for an upset stomach!
   Milk of Magnesia

10. What county is home to Strangford Lough?
    Co. Down

Round 4

1. What is the largest island in Lough Erne, Co. Fermanagh? a) Viper Island b) Cobra Island c) Boa Island.
   c) Boa Island

2. In which county did Alcock and Brown land after the world's first transatlantic flight?
   Co. Galway

3. What kind of gardens would you find on the Irish National Stud farm in Kildare? a) French gardens b) American gardens c) Japanese gardens.
   c) Japanese gardens

4. What mountains, found in Co. Laois, are one of the oldest mountain ranges in Europe? Slieve _____ Mountains.
   Slieve Bloom Mountains

5. Richard Harris, born in Limerick, is known for playing what famous wizard on film?
   Albus Dumbledore

6. Old Mellifont Abbey, Ireland's first Cistercian monastery, can be found in which county?
   Co. Louth

7. Name one sport that would have been played at the Tailteann games, the ancient pre-Olympic Irish games?
   Running, high-jumping, hurling, quoit throwing, wrestling, boxing, slinging

8. There is a festival in Roscommon every year
    celebrating what type of meat?
    Lamb

9. What town in Tipperary is the birthplace of the
    Gaelic Athletic Association?
    Thurles

10. What Waterford cyclist was the World Number
    One for six years? ___ Kelly.
    Sean Kelly

Round 5

1. How many counties beginning with 'W' are there in Ireland?
   Four

2. The Great Sugarloaf mountain is found in what county?
   Wicklow

3. What is the Irish word for deer?
   Fia

4. What date is 'Little Christmas', when the decorations are taken down?
   January 6th

5. Who is the song 'Cockles and Mussels' about?
   Molly Malone

6. In what county would you find the Newry Canal?
   Armagh

7. What is the name of the dramatic limestone landscape found in Co. Clare? The B_____.
   The Burren

8. The Mussenden Temple is the symbol of what county in Ulster?
   Co. Derry

9. What sport is Eddie Irvine, born in Co. Down, famous for?
   Formula One

10. Enniskillen is a town in what county in Ulster?
    Co. Fermanagh

Quiz

8

Round 1

1. Spiddal is the setting for what TV soap on TG4?
   Ros na ___.
   Ros na Rún

2. Which female saint founded a double monastery in Kildare?
   St Brigid

3. There is a festival in Portarlington every July celebrating what European nationality?
   French

4. *Cill Chainnigh* is the Irish for what county?
   Co. Kilkenny

5. St Peter's Church in Drogheda is famous for housing the preserved head of what Irish saint? Oliver P_____.
   Oliver Plunkett

6. The comedian Tommy Tiernan is from what county?
   Co. Meath

7. Juan MacKenna was a war hero in what South American country? Hint: You might want to bring a jumper!
   Chile

8. Which county in Connacht has the longest life expectancy in Ireland?
   Co. Roscommon

9. What influential folk band, popular in the 1960s, came from Tipperary? The C____ Brothers.
   The Clancy Brothers

10. Robert Boyle, from Waterford, is known as the father of modern: a) physics b) chemistry c) biology.
    b) chemistry

Round 2

1. What type of birds come in their thousands to the south-east of Wexford each winter? a) swallows b) geese c) swans.
   b) geese

2. What is the Irish word for potatoes?
   Prataí

3. What type of food is dulse, often eaten in Co. Antrim? Hint: It might be a bit salty!
   Seaweed

4. In what county might you hear the phrase 'That's a pink horse of a different colour'?
   Co. Carlow

5. Willie Clancy was famous for playing what instrument? a) uilleann pipes b) bagpipes c) fiddle.
   a) uilleann pipes

6. Spell 'Portlaoise'.
   Portlaoise

7. True or false: Killyleagh Castle is the oldest occupied castle in Ireland.
   True

8. In which county in Ulster would you find Lough Erne?
   Co. Fermanagh

9. The round tower in Ardmore, Co. Waterford, was built by what saint?
   St Declan

10. The comedy film festival in Waterville is named after C____ Chaplin.
    Charlie Chaplin

Round 3

1. What is the only doubly land-locked county in Ireland?
    Co. Laois

2. Lough Gur is home to the largest what in Ireland? a) castle b) passage tomb c) stone circle.
    c) stone circle

3. What well-known castle in Leinster was built for William Marshal, the 4th Earl of Pembroke?
    Kilkenny Castle

4. Oweynagat in Roscommon means 'Cave of the C___'.
    Cats

5. Carlingford in Louth has a festival every August celebrating what type of seafood?
    Oysters

6. In which county would you find the megalithic passage tombs at Newgrange?
    Co. Meath

7. What type of dairy food is Cashel Blue?
    Cheese

8. Arthur Leared from Wexford invented a type of: a) stethoscope b) x-ray c) thermometer.
    a) stethoscope

9. *Madra rua* is Irish for what sly mammal?
    Fox

10. What Hollywood actor, known for his roles in
    Taken and *Michael Collins*, comes from Ballymena
    in Co. Antrim?
    Liam Neeson

Round 4

1. What rock and roll icon had ancestors in Hacketstown, Co. Carlow?
   Elvis Presley

2. What county has won the Ulster Senior Football Championship more times than any other?
   Co. Cavan

3. Middleton in Co. Cork is known for distilling what type of alcoholic drink? a) whiskey b) gin c) vodka.
   a) whiskey

4. How many counties in total are there in Ireland?
   Thirty-two

5. Arranmore is an island found off the coast of which county in Ulster?
   Co. Donegal

6. Kippure is the highest mountain in Co. Dublin and the source of which river?
   River Liffey

7. What type of egg laid in Tuam, Co. Galway, was the heaviest of its kind?
   Duck

8. *An Lú* is the Irish for what county?
   Co. Louth

9. Eddie Macken competed in the Olympics in what

sport?
Showjumping

10. Which television and radio presenter, best known for his work with the BBC, was born in Limerick? Terry W____.
    Terry Wogan

Round 5

1. Ireland's biggest film studio, Ardmore Studios, are found in what county?
    Co. Wicklow

2. Mullaghmeen in Co. Westmeath has the largest forest of what type of tree in Ireland? a) beech b) oak c) sycamore.
    a) beech

3. In which county would you find the longest street in Northern Ireland?
    Co. Tyrone

4. True or false: storm petrels, choughs and black-throated divers are all types of fish.
    False – they are birds

5. Monaghan has one of the largest producers in the world of what natural food?
    Mushrooms

6. What film starring John Wayne was partly filmed in Cong, Co. Mayo? *The ___ Man.*
    __The Quiet Man__

7. In which Leinster county would you find the Cooley Mountains?
    Co. Louth

8. What does the Irish word *oileán* mean?
    Island

9. The Irish Fly Fishing and Game Shooting museum is in which town in Laois?
   Portlaoise

10. Peig Sayers, author of *Peig*, came from what islands off the coast of Kerry? B____ Islands.
    Blasket Islands

Quiz

9

Round 1

1. Lambay Island is found off the coast of what county in Leinster?
   Co. Dublin

2. Sir Walter Raleigh is famous for planting what vegetable in Ireland?
   Potato

3. A yellowhammer is: a) a plant b) a tool c) a bird.
   c) a bird

4. Belfast City Airport is named after which famous footballer? George ____.
   George Best

5. *Uachtar reoite* is the Irish for what cold dessert?
   Ice cream

6. Name the activity park found in the Vale of Clara, Co. Wicklow.
   Clara Lara

7. In the story *The Children of Lir*, Lir's wife Aoife cursed his children to live as what for 300 years?
   Swans

8. What is the biggest county in Northern Ireland?
   Co. Tyrone

9. What famous Irish poet spent his childhood holidays in Sligo and wrote many poems about the county? ____ ____ Yeats.
   William Butler Yeats

10. Lifford is a town in which Ulster county?
    Co. Donegal

Round 2

1. Beech, spruce and ash are all types of what?
   Tree

2. Sir Francis Beaufort was born in Navan and created the Beaufort Scale, which is used to measure: a) rain b) wind c) earthquakes.
   b) wind

3. In what county in Leinster would you find the most richly decorated High Cross in Ireland?
   Co. Louth

4. *Port Láirge* is the Irish for which county?
   Co. Waterford

5. What islands off the coast of Kerry are home to many varieties of bird, including puffins? S____ Islands.
   Skellig Islands

6. A Galway Hooker, which has its own festival in Kinvara every year, is a type of: a) bird b) boat c) cow.
   b) boat

7. Which football club plays their home games in Tallaght Stadium? _____ Rovers.
   Shamrock Rovers

8. What Irish folk and country singer grew up in Kincasslagh, Co. Donegal? ____ O'Donnell.
   Daniel O'Donnell

9. What town in Cork was the last port of call for the *Titanic*? C___.
    Cobh

10. The Galtee Mountains are found in which two Munster counties?
    Limerick and Tipperary

Round 3

1. What famous TV show about priests was filmed in Co. Clare?
    Father Ted

2. In which county beginning with 'C' would you find the Brownshill Dolmen, with the largest capstone in Europe?
    Co. Carlow

3. A pollan is a type of: a) fish b) tree c) butterfly.
    a) fish

4. *Teach solais* is the Irish for what life-saving building?
    Lighthouse

5. Yola is an extinct dialect of English once spoken in which Leinster county?
    Wexford

6. Gallybander is Waterford slang for: a) a hurley b) a slingshot c) a fork.
    b) a slingshot

7. What actor and comedian from Tipperary is known for starring in *Killinaskully*? Pat ____.
    Pat Shortt

8. What berries are often eaten at Bellewstown racecourse in Co Meath?
    Strawberries

9.   What former Irish president was born in Co. Mayo? Mary _____.
     Mary Robinson

10. True or false: Friesian cows are raised mainly for their meat.
     False – they are dairy cows

Round 4

1. In which county beginning with 'L' would you find Ardee Castle?
   Co. Louth

2. Thomas Fitzgerald from Limerick was the great grandfather of which US president? John F. _____.
   John F. Kennedy

3. What was Dame Alice Kyteler accused of being, which caused her to flee Ireland? a) a mermaid b) a banshee c) a witch.
   c) a witch

4. In which Munster county would you find Blennerville Windmill, the tallest tower mill in Europe?
   Co. Kerry

5. Who visited Galway fifteen years before he discovered America?
   Christopher Columbus

6. What Dublin town was founded by St Colmcille? S____.
   Swords

7. If someone from Donegal mentioned their 'aul doll', who would they be talking about?
   Their mother

8. What type of precious metal is mined in the
    Sperrin Mountains?
    Gold

9. In what county would you find The Burren?
    Co. Clare

10. How many counties in Ireland begin with 'K'?
    Three

Round 5

1. *Ceatharlach* is the Irish for what county?
   Co. Carlow

2. In what county would you find Coolmore Stud, the world's largest breeder of racehorses?
   Co. Tipperary

3. On December 26th, who goes around houses collecting money for a party in their town? ___ boys.
   Wren boys

4. *Deilf* is the Irish for what aquatic mammal?
   Dolphin

5. What is the oldest operating lighthouse in the world, found in Co. Wexford? H___ Head.
   Hook Head

6. What county in Munster is known as the 'Crystal County'?
   Co. Waterford

7. What Meath town has a palindromic place name (one that is spelled the same backwards and forwards)?
   Navan

8. Longford has all the native Irish species of what flying insect?
   Butterfly

9. Because the land in Co. Leitrim is so wet, people joke that it is sold by the g_____ rather than by the acre.
   Gallon

10. In which county would you find the oldest steam rally in Ireland?
    Co. Laois

Quiz

10

Round 1

1. True or false: Gowran in Co. Kilkenny has Ireland's only reptile zoo.
    True

2. What mountain range is home to Carrauntoohil, the highest peak in Ireland? M_____ Reeks.
    Macgillycuddy's Reeks

3. *Luimneach* is the Irish for what county?
    Co. Limerick

4. The wheel of which saint is the symbol of Tuam, Co. Galway? St J____.
    St Jarlath

5. John M. Synge wrote the play *The Playboy of the W_____ W____.*
    The Playboy of the Western World

6. In which county in Ulster would you find Dundonald Leisure Park, home to an Olympic-sized ice rink?
    Co. Down

7. Dana was Ireland's first winner of what song competition?
    The Eurovision

8. The English Market is a food market found in what city?
    Cork

9. What is Ireland's longest river?
   River Shannon

10. Constance Markievicz, the nationalist, suffragette and socialist, grew up in what county in Connacht?
    Co. Sligo

Round 2

1. In what Munster county would you find Cahir Castle, which looks like it is growing from the rock it sits on?
    Co. Tipperary

2. How many counties in Ireland begin with 'T'?
    Two

3. What colours are on the Irish tricolour?
    Green, white and gold/orange

4. The author Eoin Colfer from Co. Wexford is best known for writing what science fiction series? *Artemis ___.*
    Artemis Fowl

5. *Cláirseach* is the Irish for what stringed instrument?
    Harp

6. Corca Dhuibhne and Uíbh Ráthach are two Gaeltachts in which county?
    Co. Kerry

7. The shortest St Patrick's Day parade in the world takes place in the village of Dripsey in what county?
    Co. Cork

8. What county in Ulster is known as the Lakeland County?
    Co. Cavan

9. In which county would you find Lough Corrib?
   Co. Galway

10. Name the biscuit that has pink marshmallow and jam on top.
    Mikado

Round 3

1. Who was the Antarctic explorer from Annascaul
    known as the Irish Giant? Tom ____.
    Tom Crean

2. Co. Wexford is known for its flavoursome variety
    of what kind of fruit?
    Strawberries

3. Henry Shefflin from Ballyhale, Co. Kilkenny, is
    known for playing which sport?
    Hurling

4. In what county would you find the smallest chapel
    in Ireland?
    Leitrim

5. Aughnacliffe in Co. Longford means 'The Field of
    the _____': a) dogs b) stones c) bones.
    b) stones

6. Manorhamilton is a town in what county?
    Co. Leitrim

7. A red hand is the emblem of what GAA team?
    Tyrone

8. In which county in Connacht would you find the
    Yeats Memorial Building?
    Co. Sligo

9. Ernest Walton won a Nobel Prize for: a) splitting the atom b) solving world hunger c) inventing antibiotics.
   a) splitting the atom

10. What famous myth about children who are turned into swans took place on Lough Derravaragh, Co. Westmeath?
    The Children of Lir

Round 4

1. Mutton Island is found off the coast of which county in Munster?
   Co. Clare

2. Name the Cork-born footballer who has played for both Manchester United and the Republic of Ireland: Roy ____.
   Roy Keane

3. Derry is nicknamed the ___ Leaf County.
   Oak Leaf County

4. In what county is the Twelve Bens mountain range?
   Co. Galway

5. The bones of what animal were found in Poll na mBéar in Co. Leitrim?
   A brown bear

6. Who was the first female president of Ireland?
   Mary Robinson

7. What county has won more Hurling All-Irelands than any other county?
   Co. Kilkenny

8. Billy Roll is a type of: a) ham b) dance c) cake.
   a) ham

9. How many counties in Ireland begin with the letter 'L'?
   Five

10. What city in Munster is known as the oldest city in Ireland?
    Waterford

Round 5

1. In what Leinster county would you find Belvedere House?
    Co. Westmeath

2. *Cnónna* is Irish for what crunchy snack?
    Nuts

3. In which Ulster county would you find the Bluestack Mountains?
    Co. Donegal

4. Which of the following is **NOT** a type of lemonade sold in Ireland? a) red lemonade b) purple lemonade c) brown lemonade.
    b) purple lemonade

5. Bunratty Castle is in what county?
    Co. Clare

6. What type of foreign coins were found in Cloghan, Co. Offaly? a) Roman coins b) Greek coins c) Turkish coins.
    a) Roman coins

7. What is the name of the only wildlife park in Ireland, found in Cork?
    Fota Wildlife Park

8. Spell 'barmbrack'.
    Barmbrack

9. In which county would you find Jerpoint Abbey?
    Co. Kilkenny

10. Which island is the only place in Ireland to still have its own king? T___ Island.
    Tory Island